DC SUPER-PETS!™

Raintree is an imprint of Capstone Global Library Limited, a company incorporated in England and Wales having its registered office at 264 Banbury Road, Oxford, OX2 7DY – Registered company number: 6695582

www.raintree.co.uk
myorders@raintree.co.uk

Designed by Hilary Wacholz
Originated by Capstone Global Library Ltd

978 1 3982 3939 5 (hardback)
978 1 3982 4138 1 (paperback)

British Library Cataloguing in Publication Data
A full catalogue record for this book is available from the British Library.

Printed and bound in the China.

B'DG!

The Origin of Green Lantern's Alien Pal

by Steve Korté

illustrated by Art Baltazar

 raintree

a Capstone company — publishers for children

EVERY SUPER HERO NEEDS A
SUPER-PET!

**Even Green Lantern!
In this origin story, discover
how B'dg, Green Lantern of
Space Sector 1014, became
Hal Jordan's alien friend . . .**

Far from Earth, there is a distant galaxy known as Sector 1014.

Within that galaxy is a planet called **H'lven**. It is a planet very different from our own.

Most of H'lven is covered in forests. Living in these forests are small, furry creatures called **H'lvenites**.

H'lvenites look like the squirrels of Earth, but they are a totally different species. They are **super-intelligent** creatures that can speak.

Most H'lvenites are only half a metre tall and weigh about nine kilograms. They live in houses built in trees.

For years, Sector 1014 was protected by a Super Hero who came from H'lven.

His name was Ch'p, which sounds like the word *chip*. He proudly served as a member of the **Green Lantern Corps**.

This group of heroes was created to protect the universe from the forces of evil.

As a Green Lantern, Ch'p wore a **green power ring**. The ring gave him amazing powers.

With the help of his ring, **Ch'p was a brave hero**. He protected his home when it was attacked by invaders.

Ch'p also travelled to other galaxies to battle evil.

He fought beside many Green Lanterns, including **John Stewart** from Earth.

Sadly, Ch'p lost his life during a battle on the planet Oa.

With the brave hero's passing, the **Guardians of the Universe** now meet on the planet Oa.

They are going to pick a new Green Lantern to replace Ch'p.

The Guardians choose another H'lvenite. **His name is B'dg**, which sounds like the word *badge*.

Back on H'lven, B'dg is strolling through the forest.

Suddenly, a **green ring** magically appears on B'dg's finger!

A blast of light knocks B'dg over. A Guardian appears in front of him.

"We have chosen you to become a Green Lantern," declares the Guardian.

"Who, me?" says a startled B'dg.

"Report to the training centre on Oa," says the Guardian. Then he disappears.

Before he knows what's happening, B'dg magically appears on the **planet Oa**.

A small group of creatures from all over the universe stands next to him.

"Listen up, recruits!" yells a giant creature. "My name is Kilowog. I'm the Green Lantern of Sector 674. My job is to train you to become Green Lanterns."

"If you are strong and use willpower," says Kilowog, "your ring will create just about anything you can imagine."

He smiles wickedly at B'dg.

"Let's see if this little rodent is strong," Kilowog says.

B'dg gulps.

Kilowog points his ring to the sky.

Suddenly, a large, glowing green rock forms right above B'dg. Then it starts falling through the air!

B'dg points his ring at the falling rock.

B'dg uses his ring to create a giant green net. The rock tumbles into the net.

"Hmph. Beginner's luck," grumbles Kilowog.

In training, B'dg learns about his ring.
He's thrilled it gives him the power to fly.

"Wheeee!" he yells as he flies circles
around Kilowog. "I can do anything!"

But Kilowog explains that their rings have limits. They are often powerless against anything yellow.

"Yellow is the colour of fear," says Kilowog. "Only the very bravest of Green Lanterns who overcome their fears can overpower something coloured yellow."

One day, a Green Lantern from Earth called **Hal Jordan** visits Oa. He takes over the training. He asks the recruits where they come from.

"I am from the H'lven," says B'dg.

"Wow, a talking squirrel!" says Hal with surprise.

B'dg frowns. **"I am not a squirrel,"** he says. "Everyone on my planet is highly intelligent. Can squirrels on Earth talk?"

"No," Hal says. "They can't."

"Well then," replies B'dg, "Earthlings must not be as smart as H'lvenites."

A few days later, Hal leads the recruits on a long hike to a remote part of Oa.

Suddenly, a swarm of bright yellow spaceships appears in the sky. The ships fly right towards the recruits.

"Those ships belong to an evil group called the **Spider Guild**!" says Hal.

B'dg looks up at the ships in fear.

"The Spider Guild travels from planet to planet," says Hal. "After they take control of a world, **they destroy it**!"

The ships hover above Hal and the recruits.

"But the spaceships are yellow," says B'dg nervously. "We're powerless to fight anything yellow!"

CLANK!

Suddenly, a yellow chain shoots out of one of the ships. The chain circles around Hal and traps him!

The chain yanks Hal up into the air. He struggles to break free, but the yellow links are too strong.

"Run!" Hal shouts to the recruits. "Go back to the training centre and get Kilowog!"

As the other recruits start to run, B'dg stands his ground.

"It doesn't matter that Hal insulted me the other day," B'dg says to himself. **"He's a Green Lantern in danger!"**

B'dg knows that he must be brave.

He closes his eyes and holds his ring high above his head.

"I believe that I can defeat the Spider Guild," B'dg tells himself. **"No! I _know_ I can defeat them!"**

B'dg overcomes his fear!

A bright ray of green light shoots out of B'dg's ring.

The light slams into the Spider Guild ships. The ships are knocked out of the sky and crash to the ground.

The yellow chain around Hal shatters into pieces.

"You did it, B'dg!" Hal says. "You overcame your fear and saved the day!"

The other recruits gather around B'dg and cheer.

B'dg smiles happily as they all fly back to the training centre.

Later, the Guardians of the Universe gather for an important ceremony.

"B'dg of planet H'lven," says one of the Guardians, "due to your outstanding bravery, **you are now the Green Lantern of Sector 1014**."

B'dg smiles with pride. The other recruits and Green Lanterns all raise their ring hands high in the air to salute him.

Hal Jordan turns to B'dg. "When there's trouble on Earth," he says, "you are the first Green Lantern I'll be calling on for help!"

B'dg nods and says, "Hal, how would you feel about joining me on my first official mission as a Green Lantern?"

"It would be my honour," replies Hal.

B'DG!

GREEN LANTERN, SPACE SECTOR 1014

REAL NAME:
B'dg

SPECIES:
H'lvenite

BIRTHPLACE:
H'lven

HEIGHT:
60 cm

WEIGHT:
9 kg

Super Hero Pal:
**HAL JORDAN
GREEN LANTERN,
SPACE SECTOR 2814**

SUPER-INTELLIGENCE

POWER RING
Like all Green Lanterns, B'dg wears a green power ring fuelled by willpower. The ring has many uses:

CREATES ANYTHING IMAGINABLE

ENABLES FLIGHT

POWERS FORCE FIELDS

GREEN LANTERN UNIFORM
A specialized space suit for fighting evil in any environment!

HERO PET PALS!

BZZD

GREEN LANTERN,
SPACE SECTOR 2261

Super Hero Pal:
JOHN STEWART

GREEN LANTERN,
SPACE SECTOR 2814

STRIPEZOID

Super Hero Pal:
KILOWOG

GREEN LANTERNS,
SPACE SECTOR 674

VILLAIN PET FOES!

DEX-STARR

Super-Villain Pal:
ATROCITUS

RED LANTERNS,
SPACE SECTOR 666

GLOMULUS

Super-Villain Pal:
LARFLEEZE

ORANGE LANTERN,
SPACE SECTOR 2826

ORANGE LANTERN,
SPACE SECTOR 2828

B'DG JOKES!

What is a Green Lantern's favourite kind of art?
Colour-ring!

What does a squirrel say when he makes a mistake?
Aww, nuts!

What is the best way to contact a Green Lantern?
Give him a ring!

GLOSSARY!

ceremony set of formal actions and words that are done to mark an important event

galaxy group of stars and planets

imagine picture something in your mind

intelligent related to the ability to understand, think and learn

invader someone who attacks a place in order to take it over

recruit new member of an armed force

salute give a sign of respect

species group of living things that share common characteristics

universe everything that exists, including Earth, the planets, the stars and all of space

willpower strong determination to do or not do something

READ THEM ALL!

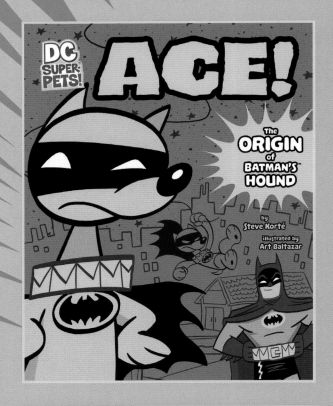

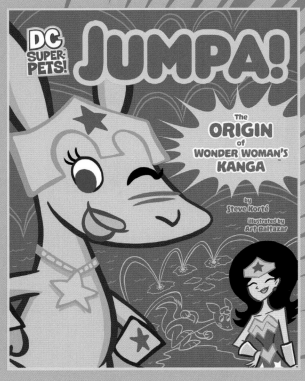

ONLY FROM raintree

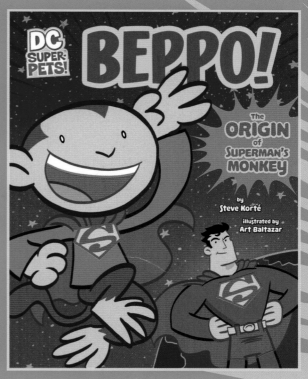

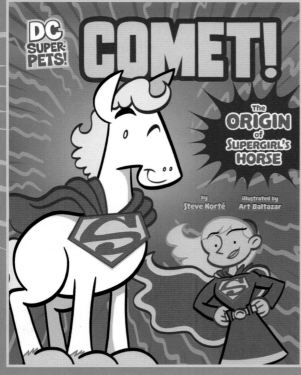

AUTHOR!

Steve Korté is the author of many books for children and young adults. He worked at DC Comics for many years, editing more than 600 books about Superman, Batman, Wonder Woman and the other heroes and villains in the DC Universe. He lives in New York City with his husband, Bill, and their super-cat, Duke.

ILLUSTRATOR!

Famous cartoonist **Art Baltazar** is the creative force behind *The New York Times* best-selling, Eisner Award-winning DC Comics' Tiny Titans; co-writer for Billy Batson and the Magic of Shazam!, Young Justice, Green Lantern: The Animated Series (comic); and artist/co-writer for the awesome Tiny Titans/Little Archie crossover, Superman Family Adventures, Super Powers! and Itty Bitty Hellboy. Art is one of the founders of Aw Yeah Comics comic shop and the ongoing comic series. Aw yeah, living the dream! He stays home and draws comics and never has to leave the house! He lives with his lovely wife, Rose, sons Sonny and Gordon, and daughter, Audrey! AW YEAH, MAN!